Where's Mommy?

By BEVERLY DONOFRIO * Illustrated by BARBARA MCCLINTOCK

schwartz & wade books · new york

Maria had a friend who was a mouse.
And Mouse Mouse had a friend who was a human.

Maria and Mouse Mouse lived in the same house
but couldn't tell anyone about each other.

If Maria's parents knew there were mice in the house, they'd get a cat.

If Mouse Mouse's parents knew their daughter was friends with a human, they'd flee to a hole in the ground.

And so Maria and Mouse Mouse kept their secret.

One summer evening, when it was time for bed, Maria slipped into her jammies . . .

. . . just as Mouse Mouse slipped into her nightgown.

Maria brushed her teeth

and combed her hair.

Mom!

she called when
she was done.

Mouse Mouse brushed her teeth

and combed her whiskers.

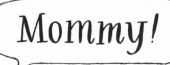

Mommy!

she called.

Maria climbed into bed.

Oh, Mom?

Mouse Mouse climbed into bed, too.

Maria got out of bed and shouted down the stairs,

Mouse Mouse got out of bed
and shouted down the hall,

In the kitchen, Maria found her
mother's coffee cup half empty.

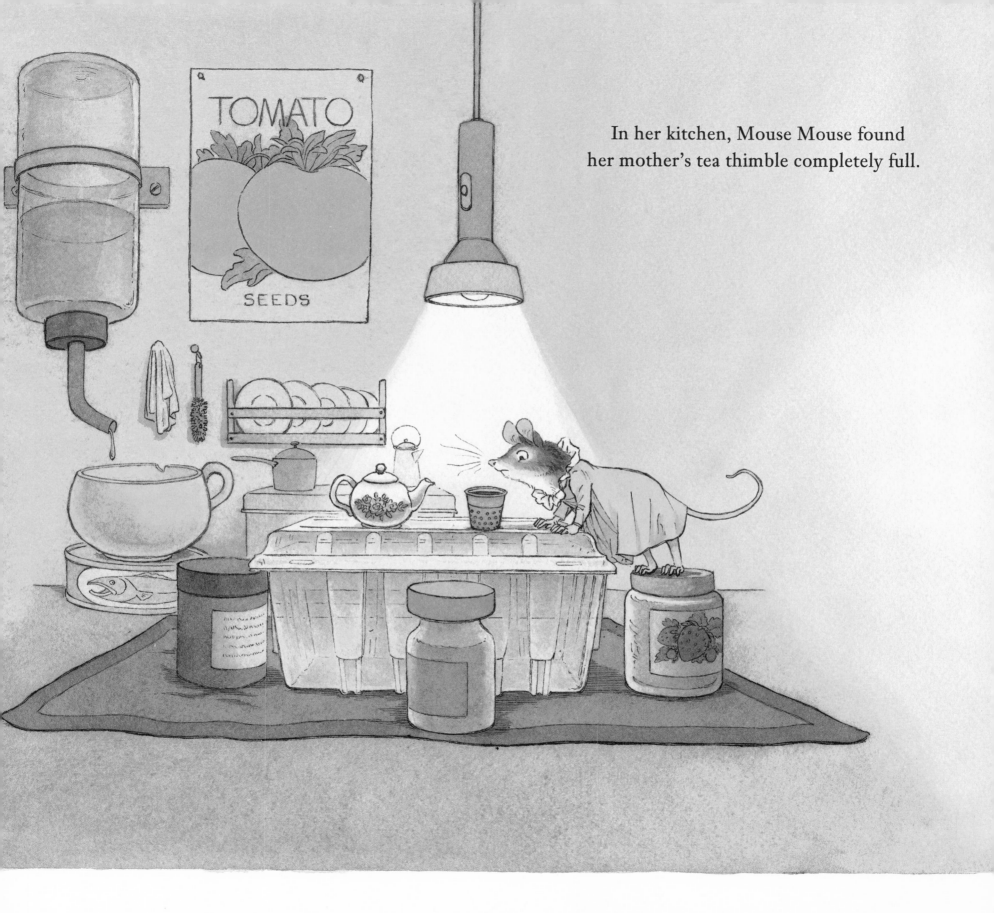

In her kitchen, Mouse Mouse found
her mother's tea thimble completely full.

Maria looked in her mother's bedroom, but there wasn't a clue.

Mouse Mouse looked in her mother's bedroom, too, but there was neither hide nor hair.

Maria scoured the living room, every nook and cranny.

Mouse Mouse even
peered behind the curtains.

Maria asked her father in the den,

Have you seen Mom?

No, pumpkin.

He patted Maria's head and
wasn't even worried.

Mouse Mouse asked her father in his workshop,

Have you seen Mommy?

No, sweet pea.

He tweaked her snout, not the least bit worried, either.

Maria didn't bother to ask her sister.
She was just a baby.

Mouse Mouse didn't bother to ask
her brother; he was just a meese.

Maria did ask her brother.

And he kept on playing dinosaurs.

Meanwhile, Mouse Mouse asked her sister,

she said, and kept on playing gummy bears.

She's disappeared!

Mouse Mouse howled.

The car was still in the driveway.
The cart was still outside the door.

But Maria's mother's sweater was
not on its peg!
And Mouse Mouse's mother's
poncho was not on its pin!

Maria's mother was not in the gazebo.
Mouse Mouse's mother was not under
the mushroom.

Maria had a feeling, and ran straight for the shed.

Mouse Mouse had the same feeling, and ran straight for the shed, too.

On the way, Maria almost tripped over Mouse Mouse. . . . Mouse Mouse ran straight into Maria. . . .

And then they both saw—

guess who!

Maria and Mouse Mouse were so
relieved their mothers were safe, and so
surprised to see they were friends, that
Maria laughed and clapped and Mouse
Mouse twirled in the air.

Then Maria walked right over and sat next to her mother.

And Mouse Mouse walked right over and sat *on* Maria.

I wanted a bedtime story,

said Maria.

Me too,

said Mouse Mouse.

So mothers and daughters, humans and mice, walked back to their house.

Each mother tucked each girl in,
kissed the top of her head,

and told a wonderful story.
And what do you think the stories were about?

For Audrey Smith Donofrio —B.D.

To David and the many mice living in our attic —B.M.

Text copyright © 2014 by Beverly Donofrio
Jacket and interior illustrations copyright © 2014 by Barbara McClintock

All rights reserved. Published in the United States by Schwartz & Wade Books, an imprint of
Random House Children's Books, a division of Random House, Inc., New York.
Schwartz & Wade Books and the colophon are trademarks of Random House, Inc.

Visit us on the Web! randomhouse.com/kids
Educators and librarians, for a variety of teaching tools, visit us at
RHTeachersLibrarians.com

Library of Congress Cataloging-in-Publication Data
Donofrio, Beverly.
Where's Mommy? /
Beverly Donofrio ; illustrations by Barbara McClintock. — 1st ed.
p. cm.
Summary: While trying to keep their friendship a secret from their mothers,
a human girl and a mouse make a surprising discovery.
ISBN 978-0-375-84423-2 (trade) — ISBN 978-0-375-94456-7 (lib. bdg.)
[1. Friendship—Fiction. 2. Human-animal relationships—Fiction. 3. Mice—Fiction.]
I. McClintock, Barbara, ill. II. Title.
PZ7.D72225Wh 2013
[E]—dc23
2011050242

The text of this book is set in Archetype.
The illustrations were rendered in pen-and-ink, watercolor, and gouache.
Book design by Rachael Cole

MANUFACTURED IN CHINA
10 9 8 7 6 5 4 3 2 1
First Edition